BLESS ME FATHER

Eamon Kelly

BLESS ME FATHER

THE MERCIER PRESS

Dublin & Cork

The Mercier Press, 4 Bridge Street Cork.
25 Lower Abbey Street, Dublin 1.

© Eamon Kelly 1977

Reprinted 1986.

ISBN 0 85342 489 6

Bless Me Father, Eamon Kelly's second storytelling show was first produced at the Peacock Theatre, Dublin on 17 June 1976. It was directed by Michael Colgan.

Printed by Litho Press Co., Midleton, Co. Cork.

CONTENTS

INTRODUCTION

STORYTELLING
An Ancient Art

As a form of entertainment, storytelling can lay claim to venerable antiquity all over the world, and also in Ireland from the time when official *seanch-aithe* told tales to kings and noblemen assembled for festivals at Teltown and Carman down to the old people of our own day in the Gaeltacht, many of whom still have a large repertoire of traditional stories but lack an audience.

An Egyptian papyrus has survived over the past four thousand years on which was written a version of the tale of 'The Twins' or 'Blood-Brothers'. It was (and is) a fine folktale, so that it spread orally over the world, and in Ireland over three hundred versions of it have been recorded. The most popular tale in Ireland was, however, that which is known to scholars as Type 300 ('The Dragon-Slayer'), which is the ancient classical tale of Perseus, and has been recorded here in almost seven hundred versions. Just as 'a good wine needs no bush' to advertise it, so a good story, which was first composed by one person in one place sometime, is usually able to survive and spread across geographical, linguistic and cultural boundaries by word of mouth, retaining its identity and yet adapting itself in details to its local milieu anywhere.

The art of storytelling is said to have reached its

highest form of expression on the lips of the Celts, the Arabs and the Slavs. In Ireland, some of the finest tales, the hero-tales, originated in the Gaelic-speaking areas of this country and Scotland, and rarely, if ever, spread to other countries. Side by side with these were tales which had originated elsewhere and, because they fitted the traditional mould, were learned and told and spread by our forefathers. The usual occasions for storytelling were the winter nights beside the fire, when neighbours came in to hear some tales told by a good narrator; the audience might consist of both active and passive tale-bearers, and all played an important role in the preservation of the art. Tales were also commonly told at wakes, as well as in fishing boats at night, while the men waited for some hours before hauling in their nets.

The decline of the Irish language and the increasing incidence of media, such as newspapers, books, radio and television, caused a lessening of the dependence of people on oral storytellers in this country and many others. Still, it is true that in many countries of the world the narrator of oral tales still has an important function, which will continue until literacy brings his usefulness to an end.

In this book Eamon Kelly, in his own inimitable way, has given a new twist to the ancient storytelling art-form. His is closest to his forbears when he narrates at length the fine tale of 'The Severe Penance' of the priest who must recover from the sea needles which have been cast into the waves. This medieval tale is an Irish ecotype of the international story, Type 756, several hundreds of

versions of which have been recorded in the Gaeltacht. Douglas Hyde published versions of this
story in his *Sgeuluidhe Gaedhealach* and in *Legends
of Saints and Sinners*.

Eamon has a wonderful natural gift of moving
on from one tale or anecdote to the next. His col-
loquialisms and comical turns of phrase add veri-
similitude to the innate humour of all the stories,
whether they tell of the apocryphal events in the
lives of Eoghan Rua Ó Súilleabháin, the Kerry poet,
or in that of the, possibly fictional, Father Mac-
Gillacuddy and his fellow-clerics — all are grist to
the mill of this talented man. Like Herodotus of
old, we may not believe that the stories are true,
but their sole purpose is to entertain us.

Seán Ó Súilleabháin.

CHAPTER ONE

THE FIRST CHURCH

In ancient times in Ireland a man was held in high
regard if he could make a verse, build a house or
tell a story, and the poet, the stone mason and the
seanchaí had permission to sit at the same table as
the king. Now, the most famous stonemason ever
to sit down with a king was the Gobán Saor and he
had a contract to build the first church for St
Patrick. The bargain was that the saint would pay
him the full of the church in grain. Churches were
not very big then. When it was finished the Gobán
Saor said to St Patrick:

'Fill it with grain for me.'

'I will,' says St Patrick, 'if you can turn the
church upside down and make a vessel of it,' thinking he had him flummoxed.

The Gobán Saor and his men got together and in
no time they turned the church upside down and
made a vessel of it. St Patrick filled it with grain
and the Gobán Saor drew it away to his own barn
and left the church upside down, and it is that way
every since!

At that time you could hardly throw a stone in
Ireland without rising a lump on a king's head,
they were that plentiful. St Patrick's idea was to
baptise the king and the rank and file would follow.
A clever plan too, only a foreigner would think of

it. It was at the building of the Tower of Babel the argument arose as to who was the king of the tradesmen, and for peace sake the foreman went around and he said to the mason: 'Who made your tools?' and the mason said, ' 'Twas the smith.' And he said to the carpenter: 'Who made your tools?' And he said, ' 'Twas the smith.' And he said to the smith: 'Who made your tools?' And he said, ' 'Twas myself.' 'That settles it,' says the foreman. 'You're the king of the tradesmen.'

There's no gainsaying it but the smith was an important member of the community and held in such respect that in places when people'd kill a cow for the tub the head would go to the smith to make soup. And prior to the vet, the smith was a horse doctor, and you wouldn't have to dig as deep in the pocket to pay him. What am I talking about usen't he pull teeth! And 'tis said there was a cure in the water where he cooled the iron. I can't think now what it was a cure for, I don't remember was it taken or applied—if it was a cure for forgetfulness, I'd do with a sup of it myself. When it came to baptising the tradesmen, St Patrick, knowing his history, called to the forge. The smith was working very hard making *cráiníns* for thinning scythes. The day was hot and he was pouring sweat, but he gave St Patrick a hearing right away for the saint's first words were:

'Come on and I'll stand to you.'

So they went across the road to the public house. The smith said he'd have a pint. St Patrick called for something temperate, a drop of cherry wine. When the pint came up St Patrick noticed that there was a good finger of froth on top of it so he

11

said to the publican:

'Here, you might as well spill a half-one into it, into the pint.'

The publican did, and when St Patrick was paying for the drink he put only the price of the pint and the cherry wine up on the counter. And the publican said:

'What about the half-one?'

'What about it?' says St Patrick. 'If the pint was full 'twouldn't go into it!'

St Patrick was good enough for him! And turning to the smith the saint said:

'Is this the usual caper, not filling the pint?'

'Oh, 'tis,' says the smith. 'No man coming in here is getting his proper measure.'

St Patrick turned to the publican and talked to him good and stiff and told him:

'Don't think,' says he, 'that you're making any profit on it. By cheating the working man you are only fattening the devil.'

The publican laughed at this. Didn't believe in it, of course, a pure pagan!

'Alright so,' says St Patrick. 'Open up that *cábúis* there under ths stairs.'

The door was opened and there was the devil inside hardly able to walk with flesh, a gloss on him!

Well, the hop that was knocked out of those there! and because of the hop that was knocked out of the publican, he told St Patrick he'd mend his ways.

'We'll see to it,' says the saint. 'I'll be calling around here again. I'm going down the country for a month.'

12

On his way back St Patrick called to the smith and he had all the tradesmen rounded up for him and a contrary bunch they were too. *Is túisce deoch ná scéal*, they say. So before the baptism they all adjourned to the public-house, and St Patrick, throwing his eye along the counter, noticed that the pints were full. Only what you may call a little christian brother's collar on the top of every one of them. He enquired from the smith if this was regular.

'Oh indeed,' says the smith, 'ever since your visit here there's a complete change in parliament. Every man coming in is getting his full measure, and what's more the publican is doing the trade of the place.'

'*Ní nach ionadh*,' says St Patrick. And going over he congratulated the publican.

'Ah, that's all right,' says the publican with a watery smile, 'but I'd like to know what effect all this is having on the quare fella under the stairs!'

'Open the door,' says St Patrick.

He did, and there was the devil inside so thin that only for the two horns you could pull him through an auger hole. If he turned sideways you'd mark him absent.

Well, the outcome of all this was that conversions were taking place with such rapidity that they ran out of salt for making holy water!

But the masons played a dirty trick on St Patrick. He was going along of a Sunday morning, and he saw the masons working. He told 'em they'd have to give up their pagan practice and keep the Sabbath, and why weren't they coming down to Mass? They couldn't they said, because

13

they had bad shoes, all white and burned from the mortar. He gave 'em the money and told 'em all to go away and buy shoes that he'd delay the bell, so that they'd be in time for Mass. They went off. You could buy shoes on Sunday for the shop-keepers were the last to be converted.

When it came to the sermon St Patrick turned around on the altar. He scanned the congregation. No masons! He was going down the town after and passing the pub he heard a great burst of hilarity. He looked in and there were the masons inside stocious on the price of the shoes. He kept his temper. 'I'll leave 'em to God,' he said. And that's why down to this day you'll never see a good shoe on a mason and another thing they'd drink Lough Erne dry!

CHAPTER TWO

FATHER MACGILLACUDDY

St Patrick never travelled on a tour of conversion
without his crozier, his mitre and his full canonicals.
And signs on it, those who followed him are very
fond of the finery. When we were small our
mouths were open back to our two ears with
wonder the first time we saw a bishop on the altar.
Such grandeur! Even out in the open at that time
the clergy went in for a bit of style. A top hat. . .
well, a three-quarter top hat. . . what we used to
call a caroline hat. You could nearly bring water
from the well in it!

Father MacGillacuddy sported a silk hat over a
flowing beard, and a fine dash he cut in a velvet
waistket and cutaway coat sitting up on the side of
a sidecar knocking sparks out of the road going
over to the chapel. Young lads playing pitch and
toss or ducks off when they heard the horse they'd
shout: 'Inside the ditch Father Mac's car is coming!'
God help any animal or mortal that wouldn't have
the agility to get out of his way. The women said
he looked very regal with the beard. They said he
reminded them of the picture of the king on the
side of the tea canister. And he was very fond of
royalty! Didn't he go all the ways up to the Cork
Exhibition and got an introduction to Queen
Victoria and to Albert to boot.

'Where are you ministering, Father?' says Albert

to him.

'Gloungreeshkeen, my lord,' says Father Mac.

'A thriving town that,' says Albert.

Father Mac did not baptise as many as St Patrick, but then again, he wasn't at it every day, only Sunday after Mass and Wednesday at three o'clock. He had stricter rules than St Patrick, and if you weren't at the chapel on Wednesday at three o'clock on the dot, you'd have a little pagan in the house for a few more days.

Timeen Sweeney from Abhanasciortán was walking in the chapel door one Wednesday at five minutes past three, and who was walking out against him but Father MacGillacuddy.

'You're late,' says Father Mac and pointing to the little child in a neighbouring woman's *gabhál*, he says to Sweeney: 'Take it home and bring it back again, Sunday.'

'God blast it! It. . . it. . . it. What "it" have you?' Sweeney was a fright for cursing—no control of the tongue.

'Blast it.' He was after coming an awful long journey. . .

'Blast it, splash the holy water on him! He won't take you a minute. He isn't the size of my fist.'
Sweeney wasn't much bigger himself and married to the tallest woman in the parish. After the marriage they were in the sacristy; of course on a morning like that a bit of levity is in order even for Father Mac:

'Well, Tim,' says he, 'when you went about it you got a fine tall woman!'

Sweeney was pure sick of these jokes and turning to Father Mac he said, 'She won't be always

16

standing, Father!'

Baptism or no baptism, Father MacGillacuddy would drive straight into town every Wednesday and straight up to High Street. He'd bring the horse skeeting on his four feet to a sudden halt in front of Thadyess's where he'd get the few commands for the week.

At that time there'd be poor men holding up the corners, only too glad of the opportunity to earn a few pence holding a horse by the head. Wasn't that how Shakespeare started in London! Father Mac would call one of these. 'Flynn! Come here and hold my horse!' Flynn would, and hold him every Wednesday, but he'd get nothing for his trouble, although Father Mac would not refuse an offering himself!

Flynn used to grumble but seeing who he was trucking with he didn't have the gumption to demand his rights, but, as the man said, constant dropping wears the stone. This Wednesday when Father MacGillacuddy drove up, Flynn walked away.

'Come here, Flynn,' said Father Mac, 'and hold my horse.'

'I will not, Father.'

'Come here, Flynn!'

'I will not,' says Flynn, 'I'm holding him long enough for you now and you never gave me nothing for it!'

'Flynn, do you hear! Hold my horse or I'll stick you to the ground!'

'Ah ha,' says Flynn. 'Why don't you stick the horse to the ground so!'

He couldn't. And why couldn't he? Because the

clergy were given no power over the animal. Over humans and spirits. Yes. They had the power there. When we were small the heart used be driven crossways in us with all the talk about the spirit of Béalnadeaga. No one'd pass that place at night. People used to go up Liosbáibe and over through Meenteogs to Gneeveguilla and Knocknagree out of pure dread.

The spirit was a woman. She was able to pull a man off a galloping horse. When she was finished with him the way she'd kill him was to give him the breast milk into the eyes. *Slán mar a n-innstear é!* She was of terrifying appearance, always enveloped in a ball of light, and one man said she came so close to him he could see the little red blood vessels in the whites of her eyes. He was lucky. He was carrying a knife with a black handle. That saved him!

She had to be banished. It wasn't Father MacGillacuddy read over her... it was another priest... I forget now what's this his name was! God knows then maybe it was a friar. It isn't everyone that can do it. And the penance he put on her was, that she would forever be, for all eternity draining the Dead Sea with a silver spoon!

'Good riddance! Didn't she attack a poor man coming home with a butt of turnips from Gloungreeshkeen! He began pegging the turnips at her in the name of the Father and the Son and the Holy Ghost. It must be the last turnip that turned the tide for she disappeared, and he fell down in a faint in the body of his car. His wife woke up when she heard the horse galloping into the yard. She knew by the crack of the axle, a frosty night, that the car

18

was empty, and all concern like at the idea of his having an idle journey she hopped out of the bed and throwing up the window said:

'John, have you the turnips?'

'Only for I having the turnips,' says he, 'I wouldn't be here!'

St Patrick never came to Kerry. How could he when the Cork people stole his donkey. He stood on a hill above Kanturk and lifting his hand he said:

'*Beannuím uaim go léir siar sibh*. I bless ye all west from me!'

How well now it was a donkey he had as his mode of conveyance! He knew about the flight into Egypt! And the entry into Jerusalem! But he might as well be idle as to be trying to show the good example to his followers. Henry Ford had no more than invented the automobile when Father MacGillacuddy had one! He was the only one in the parish with a motor car until after the second trouble. The backfiring of that instrument drove all the animals cracked. Distracted farmers hopping off the wings of sidecars taking off their coats and putting them over the horses' heads until Father Mac's car was gone.

Oh, and a reckless driver! Failing to take a turn didn't he go through Coneen Casey's gate, and knocked down a cow inside in the field. When Coneen saw the car, he couldn't get over it. He said for a thing that could run so fast wasn't it a great wonder it couldn't jump as well. He knelt down beside the cow as grief stricken as if it were his mother. The neighbours came running in. 'Is the

19

cow dead?' says Larry. 'No,' says Coneen, 'she is not dead, but she doesn't know anyone!' She didn't know what hit her!

There was a girl living over the road here—one of the Killbrains, Norry Killbrain. She was working in Cork for a while and when she came home she was up to the knocker in all the ways of the world. Powdered and painted and a Woodbine hanging out of the lower lip. Norry was mad for cars. She'd be out on the road before every motorcar. She said she loved the smell of the petrol and the lovely creaking of the leather seat when she'd sit on it. And she used be picked up too—staters and everything passing at the time.

I don't think the peepers were too good by Norry, for one day she ran out before Father MacGillacuddy, the hand up. He came to a halt in a cloud of dust like a sand storm in the Sahara. When he saw the painted hussey I can tell you she got a reprimanding. For all the notice she took of it. Standing there as brazen as you like, her two cheeks blazing, after she wetting the cover of 'The Messenger' and rubbing it into 'em.

'A nice example,' said Father Mac, 'and a nice example you are giving the young women of the parish! Is it there our Blessed Lady is? No fear. No one ever saw her smoking—in public. No. And she hadn't herself raddled with paint!'

'No,' says Norry, 'and her Son didn't have a car under his Ah either!'

CHAPTER THREE

EOGHAN RUA AND THE PRIEST

Eoghan Rua Ó Súilleabháin was mowing hay one day in the County Limerick. Poets used to have to work that time. . . and do you know they were making better songs when they were working. It was a *leaca* field and they were mowing against the rising ground, and when they put their heads over the brow of the hill they saw a big house. So Eoghan said to the local men, 'That looks like a place where a man'd get a good dinner today!'

'You are out of luck there,' the local men said, 'that's the parish priest's house.'

'What'll ye bet now,' says Eoghan, 'I'll get my dinner out of him.'

'You haven't a hope,' they said, 'but try it if you want to.'

They mowed away and when dinner time came Eoghan hopped out over the ditch, walked up and knocked at the presbytery door. The housekeeper came out.

'I want,' says Eoghan, 'to see the parish priest.'

'You can't see him now,' she said. 'He is just sitting in to the table, and he won't see anyone until his dinner is over and his punch is taken. Is it a sick call?

'It is far more serious than that,' says Eoghan. 'It is about money found lost.'

Any money found lost at that time was always

handed in to the presbytery. The housekeeper went up in the room and told the priest what Eoghan said to her.

'Don't let him go,' says Father John, 'bring him in below to the kitchen. No, no, bring him up here in the room where I can keep an eye on him.'

The housekeeper went down and told Eoghan to come in. In with him and up in the parlour and sat down to the table opposite Father John, and taking off his hat said a very loud grace in Latin. Eoghan could do it! Didn't he open a school at Knocknagree Cross! There was a big platter of laughing potatoes in the middle of the table, and another plate with more comestibles keeping it company.

Now, in olden times when a servant man was going out working for a farmer he'd say to his father on the first morning leaving home:

'Da, when it comes to dinner time how will I make sure that I'll get my full share of potatoes?'

His father would say, 'A mhic ó, when you are sitting around the table with five or six more spailpíns, and when the big ciseán of spuds is put in the middle, my advice to you, is to be eating one, to be peeling one, to have one in the heel of your fist and have your eye on another one!'

So Eoghan, being a spailpín, had good training when it came to a snapping match between himself and the parish priest for the potatoes, and he got a fine dinner. When they were finished the parish priest got up wiping his mouth with a napkin the size of a pillow-case.

'Well now my good man,' says he to Eoghan, 'and how much money did you find lost?'

'Yerra,' says Eoghan, 'I didn't find any money lost, Father. I only came in to ask your advice as to what I should do in case I did find money lost!'

Father John looking at the big pile of potato skins at Eoghan's elbow and thinking of certain remarks made by St Paul about eating and working said to Eoghan:

'There's a hundred of cabbage outside there in the haggard. Go out and set it!'

Then he rang his little bell, the signal for the housekeeper to bring up his punch. Indeed Eoghan could smell it as he went out the kitchen door. Eoghan spat on his palms, took the spade and opened a furrow straight as a die the length of the haggard. He put in the cabbage plants about half a pace apart, and put a forkful of farm-yard manure — of course that isn't what they used called it — down on the root of every plant. There was plenty of it there. The parish priest kept a cow, and then there was his own and the curate's horse.

That done, Eoghan cut a sod with the spade, turning it in to fill the furrow, and cover the base of the plant. As he went along he gave each sod a smart tap with the back of the spade to firm it in the ground. He was in great form after the feed, the sun was coming out after a shower, the birds were beginning to sing and he was in humour for composing. He was so taken up trying to get the words to run right for him that he took the spade out of the ground and was swaying from side to side in time with the tune of his new song.

In the presbytery the priest drained his glass, and walked out to see how his labourer was doing in the cabbage patch. He hopped up on a low ditch behind Eoghan. He listened for a while and then taking the note from the poet said:

> *Sclábhaí ag obair go mall*
> *Is buille aige thall 'sa bhus!*

And Eoghan turning capped it with,

> *Sagart is Laidean in a cheann*
> *Is a bholg ag damhsa le puins!*

Roughly translated what they said might sound something like this.

> *A labourer swinging the lead*
> *And the blows go sideways glancing!*

> *A priest with Latin in his head,*
> *While the punch in his belly is dancing!*

Now, any other clergyman from here to Magherafelt would have let it go at that, but Father John didn't.

Looking at the birds wheeling above him, he said:

'As you are so smart maybe you can tell me when the raven will get his speech.'

'Maybe I can,' says Eoghan, and sticking the spade in the ground and putting his shoe on the treddle, he said:

> *When Mount Brandon and Bolus will meet,*
> *And the whale on the beach takes a walk,*
> *When the clergy for gold lose their greed,*
> *It is then the black raven will talk!'*

CHAPTER FOUR

THE PRIEST AND THE PEOPLE

It is often I heard small farmers laughing as they recited that rhyme of Eoghan's, and if the truth were known it was those very small farmers gave the priests the name of being greedy. When I was young no Sunday would pass without Father Mac having to drop the hint about dues still outstanding. It was true for him when he said that it was like going to the goat's house for wool, to be going to some of those farmers for money. Men that would argue with the devil over a ha'penny on the flag-stones of hell for all eternity, according to Father Mac.

When Father MacGillacuddy was enlarging the presbytery he put a levy on the farmers of so much a cow. That was the old system and it was fair. If a man had only one cow he paid a half-a-crown, and if he had ten he paid twenty-five shillings. Father Mac left it to the farmers to say how many cows they had—he wasn't long in the parish at the time.

Two years after, when the farmers were looking to have a creamery built a cow census was taken and Father Mac was astounded at the sudden jump in the cattle population. 'Oh ho,' he said to himself, 'I'll have to be up earlier in the morning to be a match for these lads!'

When Shrovetime came round a young man from up near The Bounds was getting married and he and his father came to the presbytery to settle up with Father Mac about the marriage offering.

'Seven pounds, your reverence,' the young man said, giving a bit of *swee-gee* to the cap, 'my place is small.'

'And wet!' his father added.

'How many cows have you?' Father Mac asked him. The poor old cow was the yardstick here too!

'I have ten cows,' says the son.

'But he's only going under seven of 'em,' says the father.

'To be going under as many as seven so early in the spring is good,' Father Mac said, 'and with the help of God in another month he'll be going under all of 'em.'

Then coaxing the conversation away from the subject of money the parish priest talked to the two men about the dexter cow, and wondering what her future was like, he put his hand into the press and brought out a bottle of the hard tack. With his other hand he hauled out two glasses and half filled them, giving the father a tint more than the son, and that was a tint well spent. The father thought the dexter cow a comical animal and said if she drove milk out through her horns he wouldn't have one of 'em on his land. They were all in good humour now and by the time they got around to the bargaining again, Father Mac topped up the glasses which drove the marriage offering up too! Father Mac was as good a warrant to drive a bargain as any man that ever stood in a fair field and before the glasses were drained he had a pound a cow got out of the young farmer.

The following day walking along the village

street he said to the publican:

'Well Michael, and how much a glass are you getting for your whiskey?'

'Less than a shilling a glass, Father.'

'Ho, ho, ho!' Father Mac said. 'I got over a pound a glass for mine last night!'

Of course the clergy weren't always in big houses. In the bad times they lived in hovels, and hadn't a shoe to their feet while the parson drove around in his buggy. A man breaking stones at the side of the road said to the parish priest:

'Which of ye is nearer to heaven, Father. Yourself or the minister?'

'Oh, I'm nearer to heaven,' says the parish priest.

'It's hard to credit that,' says the stonebreaker. 'There are you without a shoe to your foot and here comes the minister in his carriage!'

'I'll go in hide now,' says the priest, 'and when the minister's carriage is passing put out your thumb and let it rub along the side of the carriage.'

The priest ducked down and the stonebreaker put his thumb up against the side of the carriage as it went whizzing by.

'Oh!' says he.

'What's wrong with you?' says the priest.

'Oh,' says he, 'my thumb is burned off me!'

'There you are now,' said the priest, 'if it is that hot on the outside of the carriage what must it be like inside!'

'Hell, Father!'

That priest had a curate and at the time they lived in a one-roomed *bothán*. The curate was a pure saint. Every ha'penny he ever got he gave it away to the poor. He would give the coat off his back to a poor man.

One morning he was coming back from an old chapel they had made of sods, and he met a beggar-man looking for help.

'My poor man,' the young priest said, 'I can't help you today.' And he couldn't for he had given away his last cent the evening before to a destitute mother to get food for her child.

'For God's sake, Father, and the sake of the Holy Angels, put your hand in your pocket,' the beggar implored.

'I'm sorry.' the young priest said, 'I have nothing for you today.'

'You won't deny the Blessed Mother, Father, for God's sake put your hand in your pocket!'

The young priest did, saying, 'Look, I'll show you my pockets are empty. There isn't a. . .' But there he found a half-crown. He knew he had no money. Not a half-crown. He had not seen one of those since the day of his ordination. There were many uses he could put it to, but he gave it to the beggar.

He came home to the one-roomed shack and told the parish priest the whole story.

'I knew,' he said, 'I had no money. Isn't it wonderful! The age of miracles is not past!'

'Ah! Miracles my hat!' says the parish priest. 'You'd want to watch whose trousers you're putting on in the morning!'

CHAPTER FIVE

CONNOR THE CARMAN

Dan Connor was a carman on the road to Cork.
He'd be car-ing butter and when butter 'd be scarce
he'd be car-ing corn. One evening he filled his load,
propped up the shafts of the car just high enough
that by rising the ridge band he could back in the
mare.

He hit the hammock early that night, and was
up in the morning before six. He hung down the
kettle and while that was coming to the boil, he
tackled the mare. That done he wet a cup of scald,
and put a fist of oatenmeal into it—it was all he
had time for. He didn't rouse the wife, they
weren't long married, and he straightened out for
Cork.

The mare had no mind for the road, she had a
foal that year and like the christian they'd be lazy
parting with their young, so that it took a lot of
coaxing to get her into her stride. They were down
as far as Mary Lyon's, that's the house with the
steps going down to it. There they met the post-
boy. He had a letter for Dan and Dan didn't look
at the letter until he had the grain sold in Cork and
the goods in the car for the road home.

When he opened it then, there was a hop
knocked out of him, for it was a letter from an
attorney in New York saying that a wealthy lady,
a connection of his mother's, had died there, and

that it would be to Dan's advantage to come over quick as there were others watching the money.

Dan, now, was a man that wouldn't let his right hand know what his left hand was doing, so he tied the mare, giving her eight to ten feet of play, to the back setlock of another car that'd be passing his own house, and told the driver to tell his wife, Nora, that he would be delayed!

He turned then on his heel and went down to Queenstown and boarded the ship for America, and at that time you'd be ages on the ocean.

When, after a few days, Dan didn't come home Nora got panicky. Carmen going the road were told to enquire about him in Cork. They did but there was no news of Dan. At that time anyone returning from the city on foot could take a nice near way across the river at Inchees. You had stepping stones there, but they were the treacherous stepping stones as many a man knew to his cost. There was a flood and a good while after a body was found in the river a mile below the crossing.

Seemingly there was a likeness, as far as a likeness could be made out, to Dan. The Sergeant said everything tallied, there was no one else missing and Dan was buried in the family ground, and his wife killed herself crying at the graveside. That was the tearful face that had many admirers, she was young, only a few months married and had the run of anything from ten to twelve cows. She was like the young widow that was bawling crying the day of her husband's funeral, and a man proposed to her.

'I can't marry you, I can't marry you!' she said. 'I am promised to the man that shaved him!'

30

Nora Connor had good neighbours, and they came together and saved the harvest, and they came together and did the spring work for her and cut the sod of turf. She came well out of it and so did the mare, no car-ing to Cork, only a bit of work around the farm and she didn't mind that for she was near the foal. *Seadh*, foal! He was a fine lump of a young colt, jet black with four white socks and a white star on his forehead, going mad with *teasbach*, clearing the five bar gate or any other obstacle until the parish priest put his eye on him.

Certain of the clergy at that time were toffs, riding with the agent and dining with the landlord. I don't know now did Father Mac bid for the colt, anyway her neighbours told Nora Connor she'd get a better price for the colt at Cahirmee fair. She wasn't short of money, no great demands to meet seeing that Dan left her with no encumbrances. She was a good catch, and signs by, after a respectable time had elapsed accounts of a match were coming to her. One man in particular had it very bad. He was a man that was trucking in cattle, they used to call him The Blocker, if you put me on my oath now I couldn't tell you what was on his baptismal certificate. We knew him only as The Blocker.

Mrs Connor was coming from town one day and she met the parish priest on the road. They were talking and he said that if she had any notion of settling down again that The Blocker would make an advisable partner for her. Well, seeing the way it was drawn down and who said it, she let the match go ahead, but the wedding was held over until the twelve months'd be up and she could get out of the black clothes.

After the marriage they were in the sacristy, talking, and Mrs Connor, well Mrs The Blocker as she was now, said to the parish priest:

'I know you have your eye on the colt and seeing you had such a big hand in today's happy event, I'll give him to you in lieu of the marriage offering. The parish clerk will be at the wedding dance tonight and he can bring the colt home with him.' Father Mac was divarted! Out with the party into the wedding drag, and drove out to Dan Connor's where everything was laid on for a right night's jollification.

'Twas dark that night when Dan Connor arrived in the big field in front of his own house. Back from America and the money in the inside pocket with a big safety pin on it. He couldn't but notice the room and kitchen all lit up, music and heluing, and shadows hopping on the screen, the wedding dance was in full swing.

Dan didn't know what to make of it. He sloped around outside lazy to go in. He put his back to the stable door where the light fell on his face. Now, this was the time the priest's clerk decided to go home and bring the colt with him. He made out for the stable, and when he saw who was there, his mouth opened to yell but no sound came out, but I can tell you he put the front door of the presbytery between him and Dan Connor in double quick time. The door of the house opened again and a bunch of strawboys came out.

'Ah, here,' says Dan, 'I'd better see what's up!' And taking one of the strawboy's hats and letting the disguise fall down over his face he walked in and asked the wife out dancing. Going around in the set he was very free-making, more so than a man should be with a newly married woman.

'Will you stop it!' said she, wriggling away from him. 'Give over! Don't you see my husband is looking! Or who are you?' she said, whipping the hat and high fiddle from his face. And when she saw who was there, she melted in a faint onto the floor. The people were dumbfounded but the music kept going for the fiddler was blind.

'What's happening in my house?' says Dan. The fiddler when he heard that took the bow away from the strings and walking in the direction of the sound let his hand run over the face.

'*Croí an diail*', he said, 'Dan Connor! He didn't change one iota!'

When the people saw that Dan was solid flesh they were relieved, and they began to hum and haw and God blast it where was he? His body was found and he was buried. That was twelve months ago and what could the woman do but marry!

Nora Connor was helped to her feet and throwing her hands around his neck she said, 'Dan, Dan, Dan, Dan, *a stór*, if you only came home a few days earlier I wouldn't have made such an ape of myself!' And consoling her he said:

'Nora, do you know what I'm going to tell you, the story could have been a lot worse if I was a couple of hours later!'

And looking at The Blocker, Dan says to him:

'Let me see your back!'

The Blocker went out the door a quiet man his tail between his legs, and do you know another man who didn't come well out of it? Father Mac, he got no colt!

33

THE PARISH CLERK

Now, Father MacGillacuddy's parish clerk was a tall graceful man falling slightly into flesh, with a soft serene countenance like you'd see on a tom cat after drinking a lot of milk. He was slow and stately in his gait as he walked the road, a straight back on him, you'd swear he'd swallowed a crow-bar, and a long black coat buttoned up to the chin. Ideas above his station! You could forgive passing strangers for tipping the hat to him. Only for he keeping out of the bishop's way people said he'd have got a parish, for he was very devout.

When the bishop was coming for confirmation, Father Mac put the parish clerk whitewashing the dry wall in front of the house. The parish clerk got his bucket and set into work making short lazy brush strokes in time with the slow air of a hymn— you'd know by him that he'd love to give out benediction!

Hail Queen of Heaven the Ocean star,
Guide of the wanderer here below,
Thrown on life's surge, we implore,
Save us from peril and from woe!

Along came Father Mac. 'Very nice,' he said, 'singing at your work and a hymn too. Very laudable, but show me the brush. Don't you think this would be more suitable,' he said as he changed

34

the tempo to:

Father O'Flynn you've a wonderful way with you,
All the old ladies are longing to pray with you.
All the young women are longing to play with you,
You have a way with you Father O'Flynn!

The bishop was very old and didn't even notice the whitewash when he came. The confirmation was held that year in the outside chapel, five miles away from the presbytery, and the bishop, because of his age, was short-taken during the ceremony, and the parish clerk brought him out the sacristy door and ducked into Hannah Maroya's. She had a contraption in the yard, the missioners used to stay there. Hannah Maroya's man that made it. He threw his hat down on the bottom of a tay chest, drew the pencil around it, cut out the hole and propped the chest over the stream in the back garden. But Hannah Maroya thought that a bit draughty for a bishop, so she said, 'Wait a minute my Lord.'

She wasn't long away, but the bishop thought it was an eternity.

'This way your Lordship.' she said and she took him down in the parlour and there, with a good sup of hot water at the bottom to knock the sting out of it, was a big chinaware pot and a blessed candle lighting at each side of it! That was respect!

CHAPTER SEVEN

THE MISSION

The darkest night that ever came in the history of the universe Timeen Sweeney went out to catch a jennet. He fell into a hole in the ground and lifting his eyes to heaven he said, 'Well may bad luck to you for a moon, you'd be out all right a bright night!'

Timeen wanted the jennet to go drawing gravel for his day's hire the time they were building the new line. It was in the middle of the winter and the days were short so that he had the dark with him going to work and the dark with him home from work. Now, this was the very occasion the government—over in London they were that time, and God knows near enough to us! — picked to bring in an act of parliament compelling the owners of all vehicles, self-propelled or otherwise, to display a light in a forward position on all such conveyances on the public highway after lighting-up time.

That was the law. Timeen had heard of it but like many country people he thought it didn't apply to himself. He was soon, as the man said, disemburdened of this idea. One Saturday night coming home tired and hungry he was held up by two well-fed R.I.C. men who wanted to know where his light was. He was in the humour for telling them that it was next to his liver, but he knew that they weren't in the humour for hearing it.

He made an excuse, that it was a new law, that he had only heard about, that he hadn't time to go to town and buy a new car lamp and that they should be lenient—it was as good-sounding word as he could think of—with him this time.

They paid a lot of heed to his pleadings! His name was taken and he was told to expect a 'whereas' ordering him to appear before the bench the coming Tuesday. He went home very upset to his wife, but she was inclined to take the long view of it. She told him to let the bad luck of the year go with it.

'Go out,' she said, 'and untackle the jennet and water him and I'll have the spuds on the table when you'll come in, Timmy boy.'

A small lunch is all he used to take to work, so that he'd have the principle meal of the day when he came home at night. Late dinner, as he used to say himself, like the quality. And a fine dinner it was too. When the wife emptied the pot of potatoes into the *ciseán*, he couldn't see her across the table with the steam rising out of 'em. She came then and landed a big plate of home cured bacon and boiled turnips in front of him, and a basin of buttermilk, a thing you'd seldom see in the winter, to wash it down. No hotel could come up with a meal like that and it would make your mouth water to see him wiring into it, for though the man was small he had a whale of an appetite. He loved the spuds. They were dry that year, balls of flour! He put a little *caipín* of butter on top of every one, which didn't get time to melt before it disappeared into his mouth. A few bulges in his cheeks as the spud came under the grinders and an up and down motion of his Adam's apple told you that it was on its way to the glory hole, and his mouth was ready for a scoop of turnips or a tasty bit of bacon. He was the picture of contentment sitting there with the traces of buttermilk leaving a white moustache on him that nearly reached half way up to his nose.

The dinner over he settled himself by the fire for a little snooze as was his wont before he'd take a drag at the pipe.

'Timmy,' his wife said to him, 'it isn't going hatching you are there, and it the closing night of the men's mission!'

It must have been the two policemen that put the thought of God out of his head. He began muttering to himself, lazy to leave the fire.

'Saturday night! What a night for closing a mission. They did everything baw-ways in the parish. I'll be late now,' he said to the wife.

'You will not,' she told him, 'if you hurry. Get out of the old duds.'

He gave a rub of the towel to his face, and put on his new coat and hat. 'It'll have to do,' he said, 'it isn't to America I'm going!'

The chapel was near enough and it looked like as if he was late for when he went out there wasn't a sinner in the street. The light in the chapel wasn't very good but he could make out the parish priest standing at the door. He was giving the tongue a rest during the mission and confining himself to ushering the people into the chapel. As you couldn't swing a cat in the porch the parish priest walked Timeen all the ways up to the front of the altar. He hadn't anchored that far up since the day he was married.

The chapel was small, the ceiling very low under the three little galleries, and with the big crowd inside in a while's time the place got awful stuffy. And we'll say now, a man with a big cargo of spuds on board. . . a man we'll say that was accustomed to take a snooze at that time every night, well, you wouldn't blame him if his eye-lids got a bit heavy.

The rosary started and Timeen survived the first decade, but half way through the second one, in the middle of a response, his tongue stopped working, his backside sagged down looking for his heels, his head dropped sideways and with his mouth open he went off to sleep. There he was lost to God and the world and the people around him wishing they were in some other part of the chapel, for their great dread was that he might commence to snore and unless he could time the snore with the response he'd be heard. A man kneeling behind tapped Timeen on the shoulder. Timeen stirred himself and half asleep sat back in the seat. Thinking he was at home he put his hand in his pocket, took out his pipe and put it in his mouth. Then he took out his penknife and half quarter of tobacco and began cutting it.

The people in the immediate vicinity went pale at the thought of what the holy Father would say if he looked around and saw a man smoking within a hen's kick of the altar. The man behind touched him on the shoulder a second time, and what did Timeen do? Handed him back the penknife! The holy Father, whose back was to the congregation, must have noticed some falling off in the fervour of the responses, for he came in with a very loud 'Our Father who art in heaven' which brought

Timeen to his senses. I can tell you when he looked up and saw the altar in front of him he wasn't long putting the pipe and the makings of the false incense in his pocket!

After the rosary came the sermon, but on the closing night the sermon is mild. There is plenty of praise in it for the people and the efforts they made to make the mission a success, but a warning note is sounded now and again about the occasions of sin. A good bit of excitement is built up during the hymns, one holy Father conducting and old lads with no more note in them no more than a crow trying to sing, *Never will we sin again!* Then comes the big blaze of candles for the renewal of the baptismal vows.

'Do you renounce the devil and all his works and pomps?'

'Oh, we do.'

'Louder!'

'WE DO!' And they were never more in earnest than the night we're talking about. I can assure you if the boyo with the horns put in an appearance he'd get a taste of his own medicine, they'd set fire to him with the candles!

Timeen Sweeney was like a hen on a hot griddle in the middle of it all. In his hurry out of the house to be in time for the mission, didn't the poor man forget his blessed candle. He was muttering to himself that the Royal Irish Constabulary put everything out of his head expecting him to have a lamp on his car.

'Here I am,' he said to himself, 'with one hand as long as the next in full view of the missioner.'

Just then the holy Father noticed him and said:

'My good man where is your candle?'

And Timeen half out of his mind with excitement at being spoken to in front of everyone said:

'Blast it, Father, that's the second time tonight I'm caught without a light!'

CHAPTER EIGHT

CIVIL AND STRANGE

Ná bí beag ná mór leis an gcléir—be civil and strange
with the clergy. Well you'd have to be, for they
were a step above the common. When I was young
you'd have only the sons of rich farmers, big shop-
keepers or professional men ordained for the home
diocese—sons of poorer men were sent foreign.
People used to remark that you'd know the farmer's
son by the way he handled his horse, and the shop-
keeper's son by the size of his name over the confessional.

My father remembered the first priest to be
ordained in our parish. I was often shown the
house he came out of. They were big farmers and
that ordination added greatly to their respectability.
In the shops you'd be left standing at the counter
until they were served. I remember the priest's
sister fine, everyone called her 'Miss'. At that time
herself and the principal teacher's wife were the
only two women facing in the chapel with hats.
That is not taking into account the tuppenny ha'
penny landlord, one of our own, that had a small
grandstand built for himself and his family at the
right hand side of the altar, so as to be away from
the commonality. His wife wore an enormous hat.

In those days to carry any weight with the people
the makings of a priest should be respectable and
fairly well to do. In their eyes riches and authority

42

went hand in hand. Signs by when the bishop had to go dipping a bit lower in the barrel for vocations, and when my neighbours heard that the son of a small boggy farmer had gone to Maynooth, by the dint of his own brains, they shook their heads and said:

'Wisha, God help us then, he'll be the priest without power!'

The old clergy had authority. Apart from a fondness for money you couldn't see any fault in their way of living. And if there was any fault the people 'd gloss it over with:

'Don't do as they do but do as they say!'

If we were to do everything they said that time Ireland would be an open-air monastery! Small children would nearly have to be imported, for the young people 'd never get the hang of things. Father Mac with a big blackthorn belting the courting couples out of the bushes and he had the full support and the sympathy of the people in that. The mothers anyway. 'My poor man. All the trouble that young crowd are putting him to. He's worn off the bones aby 'em.' Of course, to my mind there'd never be any religion in this country only for the women. The men never took to it in the same way! The women driving 'em out to confession, up to the altar and down on their knees to say the rosary. Timeen Sweeney, his mind a thousand miles away, doing eleven Hail Marys to the decade and twelve to the decade, and his wife saying, 'Glory Tim!' That was like a hul-a-hul or tally-ho to him; he'd then do thirteen to the decade!

The men sitting around my father's fire to give

you an inkling as to how devout they were. We had a holy picture up on the wall. The picture of a workshop with St Joseph cutting a big plank, and our Lord, He was only a young lad at the time, blowing the sawdust off the pencil line out before him. There was a cracked carpenter there from near Macroom, and he'd often look at the picture being in the same line of business himself. He thought St Joseph was a disgrace to the trade. A man you'd be expecting a headline from, the old traps he had. He said that saw wouldn't cut butter on a hot flag!

'If you don't give up that talk,' the women told him, 'you'll find yourself on a hot flag for all eternity.'

Eternity, according to the men sitting around my father's fire was fairly long. If a smith had a pet crow and every day after feeding him the crow wiped his beak on the horn of the anvil, when the horn was worn down to the size of a darning needle that might be the start of eternity. That was one man's idea. A second man put it this way. If you got a rock the size of Ireland and the crow wiped his beak on that every thousand years, when he'd have the rock worn away that'd be the start of eternity. But a third man wouldn't give into it. He thought the crow's droppings would add more to the rock than his beak'd wear off it. More likely he said the crow'd wind up with a big round ball the size of the world and that'd be the start of eternity!

Of course the church one time believed the world was flat! The cracked carpenter from near Macroom would never let us forget that. 'Didn't they shove Galileo into jail for saying it was round!

44

They excommunicated him!' Oh, that was a sore point with the men sitting around my father's fire, for excommunication was taking place nearer home that time. We know that absolution was always refused in the case of a reserved sin — making *poitín* or committing perjury. There was no notice taken of that, but withholding the sacraments from the men out fighting was a different thing. And they'd often tell about this man called King that was very prominent in the Land League, and in jail the time of the Plan of Campaign.

King defied the priest. He would not give up the movement. So when he was refused absolution he walked straight out of the box, and out of the chapel and never again darkened the door of it. His wife and family had to put up with hearing his name called from the altar. King couldn't be swayed — blacker he got. When there was a station in his house, he'd shake the green rushes in the yard like the palms on the road to Jerusalem, but when the parish priest walked in over the rushes, King walked out and stayed outside until Mass was over. The only place he was ever seen in the same company as the priest was at the burial of an old comrade. That would be a special day. And I suppose his thoughts would often go forward to when his own time would come, and to the class of a turn out he'd get. Well, his time did come; it will come to all of us, and his family was hoping that at the end he'd make his peace with the church and through the church with the man above. Men of influence came to talk to him. It was all of no avail. He did without 'em up to now and he'd go without 'em!'

Coming near the end his two sons used to stay up with him every night. They'd sit in the kitchen, and take it in turns to go up in the room and talk to their father. He'd be rambling in his speech and talking about the skirmishes he was in long ago. The son would remind him that those days were gone now and forgotten. 'Will I send for him?' 'No,' his father would say.

One night when the two sons were sitting by the fire, one of 'em said, 'I think I have it.' So he went up in the room and he said to his father:

'Da, what field will we bury you in?'

'What are you saying to me? I'll be buried with my people in Nohevilldaly. You know that,' he said to the son.

'Oh no, Da!' His son brought his voice down a bit because of the effect of what he said had on his father.

'If you die outside the church, Da, you can't be buried in consecrated ground. There'll be no funeral or nothing. Do you hear me?' he said when the old man didn't answer. 'Will I send for him?'

'Do whatever it is you want to do,' his father said, 'and don't be asking me about it.'

The priest came, and King died in the bosom of the church.

> *He was buried with all honour,*
> *It was a glorious sight.*
> *There were four and four more clergymen,*
> *And they all dressed up in white.*

The custom was at that time that four men of the same surname should shoulder the remains, and the man in charge called out: 'Are there four Kings there to go under the coffin?'

Four Kings! There weren't four kings left in Europe that time not to mind Gloungreeshkeen!

CHAPTER NINE

A QUIET DRINK

If two funerals are converging on a graveyard it is a common belief in some places, that the last man in will be the other man's servant for all eternity. Now that's exactly what happened the day King was burying. The other procession was seen a good bit off, and they, seeing the Kings, put on a little spurt, and the Kings too increased their pace to the point of comicality, but for all the extra effort the two remains arrived at the graveyard gate almost simultaneously, and it looked like as if the Kings were going to make it. But the widow of the other man, I forget now who is this he was, he wasn't very prominent in this life, his widow took off her shoe and hit the back left hand King under the coffin on the head. He sagged at the knees, and in the resultant disarray her husband got in first! A man is nowhere without a woman to his back!

I was coming from a funeral in Rockfield, there were three more with me. One was Dan the Dip anyway. It was very late and we coming through the town. We had enough in the same day but, there you are, the devil picked us, so we said we'd have one more *smathán* for old time's sake. It was long after hours and the public houses looked as silent as the grave. The shutters up and the lights out, and it didn't look as if we'd score.

'Well,' says Dan the Dip, 'what did we get

tongues for?' and he went around making enquiries and he got the high sign for a certain establishment, so over we went, gave three knocks on the fanlight, left a silence, two knocks, left another silence and one knock.

Oh glory, I only hope the gate of heaven will open as quick for us. There was the publican and he said: 'Don't stir a sop or a ha'port, be as still as statues.' And he let his eye wander up and down the street taking his time until he was full sure and certain there was no one suspicious at large and then he said: 'Come on in!' He shut the door, making it a big compliment, and telling us the great favour he was bestowing on us.

He put us into the front snug, and as he said himself, because of its proximity to the street he would require us to be awful silent. Which we were. There wasn't a splink of light in the snug, and someone said near me, and I nearly hopped out of my skin: 'Is that you Ned?' And who was there, judging by the voice, but Collins, a man I built a cowhouse for that same spring. I said: 'The devil fly away with you, Collins, and the start you knocked out of me in the dark!'

Well, I don't know, it is next door to impossible to carry on any business in the dark, where money has to change hands and pints of porter have to be filled out. But along came the publican and he had a candle lighting under the mouth of a canteen so that there was only a circle of light going on the floor, the naked flame not exposed, for it could go through a crack in the shutter and the police passing outside'd see it and the fat'd be in the fire.

He brought us the drinks and by then my eyes

were getting accustomed to the place and I looked in through the cubby hole to the bar, and there was a fair scattering of people inside. They were talking away very low, a sort of rumble it would remind you, for all the world, of the buzz of blue bottles trying to get out of a butter box. I introduced, having my manners, Dan the Dip and the two lads that were with me to Collins and he had two fly-by-nights in his own company, and he introduced them to us.

We were putting out our hands in the dark in the direction the voices were coming from, I know, I nearly got the eye knocked out of me and I wound up shaking hands to myself!

After all the warnings we got to keep quiet, you'd forget, and we got a little bit loud and the publican used to come every now and again, as he said himself, to admonish us. He was very precise in his speech and why not he? A brother a doctor over in England, another brother holding down a parish in Nebraska and a son in the police in Singapore. I tell you there's money in drink!

After a couple of jorums—the lubrication can have an effect on the tongue, it will loosen the hinges—we got awful loud and Collins was the loudest for he was a bit of a blackguard.

'Did you ever hear Ned,' says he, 'that this barber next door used to go down to the palace every morning to shave the bishop? This was a regular commitment and the bishop was lucky, for he was a good barber, as good a man as ever learned his trade, until he took to drink and in time it began to show in the hand.

The bishop saw it, but the barber was so long

shaving him that they were used to each other, and he didn't want to be making changes bringing a new man into the palace, maybe to be taking stories out of it. One morning after a hard night the barber lathered the bishop. The bishop would have his eyes closed for that, and when he opened them he noticed that the shake in the barber's hand was very bad. There was nothing for it now only offer it up! When the job was done the barber held up the looking glass, and the bishop saw small little oozings of blood all over his face, and throwing his eyes to heaven he said: "Oh, God, isn't drink a fright!"

"That's right, my Lord," said the barber, "it makes the skin very tender!"'

There was a loud guffaw. And when you are not supposed to laugh it is the very devil to keep it in. We were shoving the caps in our mouths to hold back the great *tulc* of laughing, and Collins, enjoying the state he had put us in, gave vent to a loud he-haw an ass needn't be ashamed of!

The publican came charging out and said to Collins:

'God man, you'll be heard in Gullane, and remember you are not a customer in this establishment. I strained a point to let you in here!'

'Well now,' said Collins giving him the glass, 'go away and strain another one!'

Very good why. At this minute the publican's wife came running downstairs. She was on an L.O.P. at the top window, and she said that there were two guards passing Hanaffin's. We cocked our ears and sure enough we could hear the pounding of the two pairs of feet good and slow and solid approaching nearer every second, and when they were coming to the door we held our breath waiting to see would they halt. No, they passed on and they were barely out of ear shot when Collins settled into:

When a the roses bloom again down by the
river

'Shut up Collins! Put a sop in it!'

And a robin redbreast sings his heart's refrain!
For a the sake of old langsyne,
I'll be with you sweetheart mine
I'll be with you when the roses bloom again!

With that there was a frightful pounding at the front door. And the publican said labouring up from the bottom of the throat a nice tone:

'Who is they-ur?' You'd think he was talking to a bishop. 'Who is they-ur?'

'Guards on duty, open up!'

Well, the publican got frightfully excited, he had been caught a few times before and the licence could suffer.

'Look,' he said, 'I am inviting you all up to the parlour. There, take a bottle of stout every man of ye. Say I gave it to ye and remember we are arranging an outing and I am going too. Upstairs quick!'

As himself and the wife cleared the counter of porter stained glasses we pounded up the stairs. Collins was the slowest for he was almost legless. We got into the parlour where it was fine and bright, but I couldn't get 'em to settle down so that we could prepare what we were going to say to the Sergeant. There they were staggering around examining the knick-knacks on the what-not and looking at the photographs on the wall. There was a big photograph of the publican's brother, the doctor, another stylish one of the Nebraska parish priest, not to mind the Singapore policeman in full regalia.

We were only barely sitting down when another uniformed figure appeared at the top of the stairs. It was the Sergeant and looking around he said:

'Can ye account for yeerselves now. Can ye account for being on licensed premises after hours?' I said: 'We were invited.' Well, we were invited upstairs anyway!

'And what about the refreshments?' Dan the Dip holding the bottle to his heart told him: 'The publican stood us that.'

'Fair enough,' the Sergeant said, 'but explain to me now about this outing!' There was no answer. He looked at me and I said: 'We are going on a pilgrimage.'

Letting his eye ramble around the room and taking in the state of the company, he said: 'I didn't know there was a pilgrimage to a brewery! Where are ye going?'

'To the Reek,' I said. 'We are going to Croagh Patrick.' And I was very sorry after for having said it, for I knew if he questioned the people there some of them wouldn't even know what county the Reek was in. We told him then, and the publican joined in, that we were making plans whether we'd go by train or take the bus, where we'd stay the night before and so on.

Everything was working out fine, and even

though it was unusual for people from our locality to go to Croagh Patrick the Sergeant believed it for he shut the book. The relief on the publican's face was plain to see as the Sergeant made for the door. Now all would be honkey-dorey only the Sergeant paused to have a word with the publican's wife on the landing, and Collins thinking he was gone gave vent to a drunken guffaw. ' 'Twas a bloody great plan!' says Collins. 'An outing to Croke Park! He believing we'd go all that way when we could hear the match on the wireless at home!'

Collins never put his leg across the threshold of that establishment again.

CHAPTER TEN

THE POOR SOULS

There was this man Malachi Dhónail and he could read with the priest and out-do him in power. The same Malachi had power over animals too. If he didn't like you he could put a plague of rats on your house the rats'd do his bidding. Some strangers were in Malachi's kitchen one night and down near the dresser they noticed two rats sitting on the edge of a pan and they wiring into the hen's mess. And sitting on the table was this big hoor of a white cat and he blinking at 'em. The strangers couldn't get over the unnaturalness of the cat's behaviour, so one of 'em said to Malachi:

'What's wrong with the cat?'

'Ah,' says Malachi, 'you should see him if a strange rat came in!'

Malachi would never get involved with the clergy only when he had drink taken. He was one day standing in the chapel-yard arguing with the priest. There were two pigeons perched on the gable of the chapel.

'Come on now,' says Malachi to the priest, 'which of us will have his bird down first!'

They began to read and in a while's time the two pigeons came tumbling down.

'Now,' says the parish priest, 'my bird was down first.'

'Yes,' says Malachi, 'but mine is fit for the pot.'

There wasn't a feather on Malachi's bird. The priest walked into the bottom of the chapel. Malachi followed him in and bringing his voice down a peg, by the way out of reverence, he said to the priest:

'Come on. I challenge you by the dint of reading to light a candle on the altar from where we are standing.'

'Come on,' says the priest, wouldn't you imagine he'd think more of the cloth. 'Come on then.'

Well, they began to read and in a while's time a little flame appeared on the candle on Malachi's side of the altar. It began to flicker, but he fed the words to it and it blazed up into a fine strong flame. Over at the priest's side of the altar a little light appeared on the candle. It began to flicker, spluttering up and then went out. There was a little puff of smoke as a red spark died on top of the wick.

'What happened to me?' says the priest.

'You went astray,' says Malachi, 'in the reading of one syllable. It was as tight as that!'

'You are an evil man,' the priest told Malachi, 'and it is by the power of darkness you lit that candle. You'll come to a bad end. You'll die in drink!'

'I won't go unknown to you,' said Malachi.

And sure enough Malachi, in a drunken state, stumbled into a stream. He was found face down there, and the old people said that the instant the soul left his body the gable of the chapel fell in!

By the same token I was in a public house in Baile Mhúirne. I was stranded there of a night. There must have been five or six of us in the back

56

snug and we were having a discussion as to the size
of the human soul. We were fairly far gone! One
man said it was so small you could hold it in the
cup of your two hands. He made a little cage with
his cupped palms, and moving his thumb he put his
eye to the opening and began to describe the soul
to us. He said it was like a small bright bubble with
a little pulse in it, about the size of a little *peidhleachán* with red dots in what looked like wings. If
you lifted your thumbs it would fly away.

And he told us about this soul, it was a lost soul,
it was in total darkness and was clinging to the
back of an ivy leaf. There was no sound ever in the
dark except maybe the ivy leaf flapping in the
wind.

One time the soul heard someone laughing and it
said: 'Who is that?'

And wasn't it another soul at the other side of
the ivy leaf.

'How long are you there?' says the first soul, and
the second one said: 'Three times three score years.'

'I'm here far longer than that,' the first soul said,
'I've lost all track of time, but tell me, why were
you laughing there now?'

'Because I heard good news,' the second soul
said. 'Just now wasn't there a son born to the son
of my son's great-grandson, and when he is twenty-
two years of age he'll be ordained. And at his first
Mass he'll remember all those of his own family
gone before him and that morning I'll be free! Did
you hear me?' he said, for the first soul didn't
answer.

'I did,' he said, 'fine for you. I've no one belonging to me.'

'Have courage,' the second soul said. 'Do you know what I'll do? Whatever good is coming from that first Mass I'll go halves in that with you!'

Our Lord and His Mother were out walking above and she says to Him. 'Did you hear that, hah?'

He said, 'I did, what about it?'

'To think,' she said, 'that that lost soul after waiting so long for his release, and then when the means of his release comes he's willing to share it with a complete stranger. What are you going to do about it?'

'Well, I suppose,' says He, 'for peace sake I'll have to do something!'

She went away and put the sheets airing, and that night St Peter had two more Baile Mhúirne men in heaven!

CHAPTER ELEVEN

THE SEVERE PENANCE

There was this man and he had three sons, and when it came to the time for him to settle up his affairs, to his eldest son he gave his house and land, to his second son he gave his passage across the sea and to his third son he gave enough money to get him through college to be a priest.

The third son set out; there were no roads or railways in Ireland then, and he kept going, lodging a night here and a night there, until at last he came to the college which was somewhere near Athlone. Five years he gave there until he was turned out a fully ordained priest. He got ready then and he put his books in his bag saying:

'I must go home now and see my mother and my father and thank them for all they have done for me.'

He set out and he walked all through the day, and when darkness was falling he saw a light that way from him. He went towards it and saw that it was a rich man's house. He walked into the yard and he asked for lodgings.

'You can have a bed here and welcome,' the man told him, and indeed that man didn't know what to do for the young priest he had such a high regard for him.

The young priest was a fine figure of a man, and the daughter, as you might say, put her eye on him when she brought him in his supper, and a fine supper he got. When they were all in bed that night the young woman came into the room where the young priest was. She wanted him right go wrong to give up the church and marry herself.

'A handsome man like you,' she said, 'throwing away your life.'

She was an only daughter and she told him that.

'And we'll have this fine house,' she said, 'and all that's going with it if you marry me.'

'Don't be telling me your mind,' he said, 'for it is no good. I have my vows taken. I'm satisfied with that, and I can't ever marry.'

She gave it up then when she saw it was no good for her. But in a while's time she came back again to the room where the young priest was. He was asleep now and she put a gold plate belonging to her father between the books in his bag and out with her.

When the priest got up in the morning he was readying himself for the road. He put his coat hanging that way on the door while he was washing his face. Unknown to him the young woman came and put a piece of cold roast beef in his pocket. Now it was Good Friday and she didn't offer him any breakfast. Even in a rich man's house, at that time, Good Friday was black fast.

When he was a couple of miles from the house, she went and told her father that the man who stayed the night was gone and that the gold plate was missing. Her father saddled his horse and it wasn't long until he overtook the priest.

'You looked like an honest man,' her father said to him. 'Little did I know I was harbouring a thief!'

The young priest was brought before the jury. Her father showed them the bag, they opened it and there sure enough was the gold plate. There was only one punishment for a thief at that time, so he was sentenced to be hanged. When he was up on the stage and before the rope was put around his neck, he was given permission to speak. He told the people who he was, that he was on his way home to see his father and mother, and that was how he came to be in the rich man's house.

'That young woman there,' he said, pointing her out to the people, 'wanted me to marry her, but I couldn't give in to that. I don't know,' he said, 'how the gold plate came to be in my bag or how the fish came to be in my pocket.'

'It wasn't fish I put in your pocket,' she said, 'it was roast beef.'

She should have kept her mouth shut, for the jury began to cross-hackle her and in the end she had to admit that she put the gold plate in his bag. Now in everyone's eyes her crime was as bad as that the young priest was supposed to have done, and the jury said there was no way out of it only hang her. When she was mounting the stage she said to the young priest:

'As sure as there's a God in heaven you'll be the sorry man yet!'

He came home and he saw his people and after a while he was allotted a parish. He was happy and contented and he had the respect of everyone. All was fine until one day he was on a visit to the landlord. The landlord had a fine garden near his house and the young priest was walking there after a good dinner, reading his office, when a young

61

woman came up to him. He didn't know her and thought she was someone connected with the house. She was ever so forward and freemaking and began linking him around the garden. Now, that way in a quiet corner there was a sun house. He ran into it to be out of her road but she went in after him. And it seems that by the dint of sweet talk she turned his head and the young priest forgot himself.

When they were parting the young woman said: 'You ought to know me! I'm the woman you hanged. I came back to blacken your soul!'

He was a sorry man now, and he wasn't getting any peace of mind day or night, so he went and made his confession to the bishop and the bishop told him he was damned.

'There's no hope at all for me?' said the young priest.

'There's no hope at all for you,' the bishop said, 'unless you take this bundle of needles and get a boat and put to sea, and as you row away, every hundred spades throw out a needle until the last needle is gone. Then unless you are able to gather up all those needles and bring them back to me you are lost for ever!'

'I'll never see your face again,' the young priest said, 'for that's an impossible thing to do.'

But he got the boat, and he put to sea and as he rowed away, every hundred spades he threw out a needle, and when the last needle was gone so was his strength for he had no food or no drink. He was three days then under the heat of the sun, and on the evening of the third day he saw land.

He made towards it and put ashore. He walked

for a while and when darkness fell he was in a big wood. He saw a light, he drew near it, and there he found a house and around the fire were twelve children. He asked them for something to eat and they gave him his supper.

He told them his story and about the cruel penance that was put on him by the bishop, and he asked them if they could at all, to tell him of any person he could go to that would save him from the terrible consequences of this penance.

'We don't know,' the children said, 'but for the next three mornings at six o'clock a monk is coming here to say Mass. If he can't save you, no one will.'

The young priest went to bed. Every bone in his body was aching after the long journey, and he fell into a sound sleep. When he woke he asked the children did the monk come yet?

And they said: 'Mass is over and the monk is gone!'

He was so heavy with sleep that day he could hardly keep his eyes open, and so that he'd wake in time for Mass the second morning, he slept that night on the cold flags of the floor. When he woke he asked the children if the monk came yet?

'Mass is over,' they told him, 'and the monk is gone.'

He was in great dread now that he would miss Mass the third morning, so he went to the wood and cut down a thorn tree. He made a bed of it, and when night time came he took off his shirt and lay on the bed and the thorns bit into his flesh and kept him awake until the monk came. When Mass was over the monk was leaving and the young priest went up to him and said:

'Don't go awhile. I have something to tell you.' And he told the monk all he had been through since the day he was ordained and about the penance put on him by the bishop and what he would have to do if he was ever to see his home again.

'Tomorrow,' the monk said, 'you will go into the nearest town, and go up to such and such a street where you'll see a woman selling fish. Take the first fish you'll lay your hand on; that fish'll be fourpence and here's the money. Open the fish and take out what's inside, but I implore of you put the fish back in its place!'

Next morning the young priest went into the town and kept walking until he came to the place where the woman was. He took the first fish he laid his hand on and paid the woman. He opened the fish and there inside were the needles.

He left the fish with her and came back to the house. The children got some food and drink ready for him, and he turned his face towards home. When he landed he pulled the boat up on the shore and made off to his own house.

When the bishop heard he had returned he came to the young priest.

'I can't believe it,' he said, 'that you are back. Have you the needles?'

'There they are there,' says the young priest, 'you can count 'em.'

Now it was the bishop s turn to be uneasy in his mind and he was getting no peace day or night, so he said he'd go to the Pope. He made his confession and he told the Pope about the penance he put on the young priest and how it turned out.

When he had finished the Pope reaching that way above his head took a parcel down from a shelf and giving it to the bishop he said:

'You wronged a good man.'

The bishop opened the parcel and it was full of needles. He went then and he got a boat and put to sea, every hundred spades throwing out a needle.

But the bishop never came back!

CHAPTER TWELVE

EOGHAN'S SCHOOL

Eoghan Rua Ó Súilleabháin had a school too, though it was not as big as the one near Athlone. Eoghan's school was at Knocknagree Cross, Father Ned Fitzgerald that opened it and Father Ned Fitzgerald that closed it. I remember enquiring when I was small why Father Ned did that. The old people didn't know, though one man with a glint in his eye wasn't long giving a reason for it.

He said Eoghan was a hard man for the women. Like Diarmuid, Eoghan had the *Ball Seirce*, no load to any man, and the attraction being there the women were mad about him. At wake or wedding or anywhere you'd have good looking women, Eoghan would be planked down in the middle of 'em. Like that Eoghan was one night at a wake surrounded by a prize bunch of merry women. Whatever caffling was going on one woman made an indelicate sound, a small report, but loud enough to be heard.

Then all the women began to laugh and nudging each other said, 'Ah ha dee, Eoghan!' by the way blaming it on him.

'What's natural,' says Eoghan, 'can't be remarkable, but I'll bet a pound to a ha'penny I'll find out which of ye ruffled the air!'

They had a fine piece of innocent fun blaming each other and blaming Eoghan. The clay pipes were being handed out, at the time the women smoked too, and they were in a circle around the blazing splinter waiting their turns to get up steam. They had to be careful reddening the pipes from that thing or they could set fire to their headgear. Eoghan left 'em alone for a bit and then of a sudden he said:

'The lady that "killed the cat" her dandy cap is on fire.'

A pair of hands went up to a head giving the game away, and realising the trick Eoghan played on her she went to give him a good humoured thumping and wound up rolling in his arms — a thing she didn't find any fault with!

But to come back to Eoghan's school, English was making its appearance in Sliabh Luachra at the time and the well-to-do, there weren't many of them there, believed English was the coming thing that you couldn't get on without it. The mothers liked their daughters to be precise in the new language, pronouncing it to a 't', able to give an account of themselves when they went into Killarney, and of course it would also improve their marriage prospects. So they sent their daughters, big grown women down to Eoghan's school at Knocknagree Cross to get a good grounding in grammar. Now, Eoghan's grammar school was a continuation of a hay-shed, and it seems Father Ned Fitzgerald paid a surprise visit and found Eoghan on a bench of hay with one of these young women. As the man said that told me the story, 'She could parse but not decline!'

It wasn't the end of the world that time if you lost a job like school-mastering, you could turn your hand to the spade, the reaping hook or the *grafán*. As well, a poet like Eoghan could turn a few bob by making up a praising song for the well-to-do. Eoghan was still a young man when he made a song of praise for one Daniel Cronin, when the same Cronin was made lieutenant of the horse soldiers in Killarney. The song was in English, which was what Eoghan thought might suit in Cronin's case. Cronin never paid Eoghan for the song nor even let on he got it, which was nothing short of an insult.

Eoghan was one night in a public house in College Street and Cronin's name came down. If it did Eoghan gave him the edge of his tongue — said he was the seed, breed and generation of *ceithear-nachs*, which I suppose he was. Unknown to Eoghan some of Cronin's retainers were in the house. One word borrowed another until they came to blows. Now Eoghan could give as good an account of himself as any man in a fair fight, but he didn't get a chance. One of Cronin's servants, a treacherous crew, picked up the tongs and cracked him on the head with it.

He was brought to Knocknagree, every care his friends could give they gave it, there was no medical attention at the time. It was heartbreaking for them to think that one so full of life should go. His friends couldn't accept it that there was any danger. They coaxed a young woman to go into the bed with him. It was no good. He fell into a fever and died. No one knows rightly where Eoghan is buried but the day of his funeral Father Ned Fitzgerald said that he was a fine christian man.

CHAPTER FIFTEEN

THE GOLDEN BALL

Guirteen was living in the townland of Lyre. He was alone there in the house for he never married, he was too shy when he was young and too old when he got the courage. He had a great liking for mushrooms, and he'd be out with the crack of dawn in late June walking barefoot through the dewy grass.

This morning as he went along his toe struck a bunch of growing rushes, and a little gold ball hopped out to him. He put it in his pocket and brought it home, and he was looking for some safe place to put it to keep, for it was a nice nest egg to have!

Now, for all the world that was the time he had the stone mason building the new chimney and in all old fashioned hearths, you had a square hole left in the pier where the man of the house could keep his pipe, or the woman her tay canister.

'Do you know,' says Guirteen to the mason, 'that *cábúisín* is only gathering place for dust, and my advice to you is to close it up.'

The mason was dressing down a square flag for the mouth of the cubby-hole, and when his back was turned Guirteen buried the gold ball in a lump of mortar and threw it into the hole, and the mason put the flag in position and plastered it over to 'match existing wall'.

In a while's time Guirteen went out to the haggard and what did he see there but a lovely young woman. He asked her who she was, and she said she was Mary O'Sullivan from the west of Kerry.

'You're a fair step from home so,' he said, and he wanted to know what message she was running in that part of the world.

'I'm going in service,' says she, 'to a big farmer in Shanagolden, but I'm afraid I'm gone a bit off my road.'

'You are,' says he. 'I'm very short handed here, being alone and that, and if you'll come working to me I'll give you whatever wages you're expecting below in Shanagolden.'

There wasn't another word said, and no better servant ever came inside a man's door, to bake, to boil, to wash, or sew. She left the sign of her hand on the house — and indeed it needed it! But there was one thing, if Guirteen ever came in unexpected from the fields he'd always find her rummaging on the top of the dresser, along the thatch or behind the bin; and this day she was above in the loft with the tin trunk thrown sideways, and she going through the contents of it. Guirteen never tumbled to what she was searching for. How could he for he had something else on his mind.

She didn't go home at all for Christmas, and he didn't remark on it, not knowing how she was situated with regard to her people. Shrovetime came, and do you know it was younger Guirteen was getting, and no day went that he didn't throw on the collar and tie. This night the two of 'em were talking by the fire, and he said:

70

'Well now Mary, you can't but know the extent of my farm and buildings and it isn't like another house, you'll have no relations to be playing with, so would you marry me?'

'Not at the moment,' says she, and placing her hand in his she said:

'You must have patience, that's what you must have.' He curbed his tongue, though 'twas hard for him, and reaching up for his fiddle he played her a tune:

> *Ar maidin inné sea do dhearchas an stuaire-*
> *cailín,*
> *Her limbs were complate and she nately*
> *clothed in green,*
> *A malla ba chaol is a béilín ba ró-mhilis bhí,*
> *And I knew by her gazing she'd play the hide-*
> *and go seek!*

Faith! She remained on in the house with him after that, and as the days lengthened out into spring anyone living in the place and keeping his eyes open could see that she was still searching. She went from the house to the out-offices, and from the out-offices into the open and every loose stone she turned, even the rusty bucket with the dock leaf growing up through the broken bottom, she'd knock sideways to see what was under it. She tried every hole and corner and as time went by the colour left her cheeks and she pined away till she was only a bare shadow of the Mary O'Sullivan that stood in the haggard the June before.

Everything that could be done was done, but in spite of all she died.

Guirteen waked her the same as if she was one

of his own, and at that time the wake'd run three nights and the corpse'd be laid out on the kitchen table, and every night the house was full.

The first night coming up to twelve o'clock the horse's hooves came pounding into the yard. The door burst open and in came a strange man of pale appearance. He walked up and stood over the corpse and said:

'*A bhfuairis an rud úd abhí á lorg agat?* Did you get that thing you were searching for?'

And the girl said:

'I did not nor a sign of it,' and fell back on the table.

Cold sweat stood out on every forehead as the stranger went out the door and they heard the horse galloping out in the yard — I tell you no one went home after the rosary that night! They held on, and when day broke, they were so drowsy and upset that they thought it was how they dreamt it. But when the same thing happened the following night the men put their heads together, and one of 'em was for going with the first light to the presbytery.

'The wrong move,' says Guirteen, 'the only thing that'll come out of it is another sermon about drink at wakes.'

'What'll we do so?' says they. 'Here we have a riddle that we can't unravel.'

'Well,' says Guirteen, 'Malachi Dhónail is known to everyone of us and from his talks with the old people he can't but have an inkling into things. He was a long way on the road to ordination, and can light a candle on the altar by the dint of reading.'

Malachi Dhónail was seen in the morning and he

said:

'I'll come along to that wake tonight.'

He was sitting among the men in the kitchen, when coming up to twelve o'clock the saddle horse galloped into the yard. The door burst open and in came the same man of the two nights before. He walked up and stood over the corpse and said:

'Did you get that thing you were searching for?'

'I did not nor a sign of it,' the girl said, and fell back on the table. The stranger moved to go.

'Now lads!' says Malachi and like lightning they were between the stranger and the door and holding up his hand Malachi said:

'I command you to give an account of the commotion you have created in this house for three nights running.'

'I was waiting for someone to ask me that,' says the stranger, and looking around the kitchen he said:

'I'm not one of ye! I'm from the other world. Our game there was hurling, and we played it under the full moon in that field below, but we've no game now, and all because of that girl lying there. Her job was to stand on the sideline and watch the ball going wide, but she neglected her duty and lost the golden ball and there'll be no peace in this house till we get it!'

'Where's the spawl hammer!' says Guirteen racing around the kitchen. He found it and smashing the flag in front of the cubby-hole, he took out the golden ball and threw it to the stranger. He rubbed the mortar off it on his sleeve till it glittered.

'Ah ha,' says he, 'this is it, our hurling ball!' and motioning to the corpse he said:

'Come on! We'll be going!'

'You're going,' says Malachi, 'but she's not! Or do you mean to stand there and tell these people that any girl that lived so long in this house where she was every day in contact with the fire, is one of ye! Isn't she a changling!'

'She is,' says the stranger, 'we have to have a go-between.'

'Well, I command you,' says Malachi, 'to clear the cloud from her mind and restore her to normal life.' The *joeyman's* face blackened with the dint of bad stuff, and muttering some words he filled the house with a whirling noise, there was a burst of light and like that the dead girl hopped off the table and stood there every bit as lovely as she was in the haggard the June before.

The man was gone for they heard the horse knocking sparks out of the paving stones in the yard. Guirteen was the first one over to the girl's side and taking her by the two hands he said:

'You're a free woman now, Mary, and I suppose you'll go back to your people. Why then, the two of us were happy in this house, and I made bold enough to ask you a certain question one time when you were under the spell.'

'Ask me again,' says Mary, 'and see what I'll say!'

He asked her again and she said she would, and what began as a wake ended up like a wedding!

> There was gaiety where grieving was,
> Music where mourning was,
> Singing where *caoining* was,
> And the rafters rung till the sun peeped in the window.

74

CHAPTER THIRTEEN

THE STATION HOUSE

'In the name of the Father and of the Son and of the Holy Ghost. Amen. The following are the stations for the coming week. Tomorrow, Monday for the townland of Craughatusane in the house of the representatives of the late Jeremiah Tagney. Tuesday, for the townlands of Shrone and Meanageshaugh in the house of Laurence. . .' There was a station published for Larry one time. He was a relation of my own, a man that lived to be nearly ninety years of age and was only one week sick in his life — that was the week he died of course! I don't remember this too very well myself now. The old people I heard talking about it, and what kept it so fresh in their memories was something comical to take place the morning of the station.

The station goes back to the penal times when people of Larry's persuasion had to worship in holes and corners. And the station, as we were often told from the altar, is the morning when the kitchen becomes a sanctuary and the room becomes a confessional. Indeed Larry's room wasn't much bigger than a confession box. But the kitchen was enormous. Paved floor, except that there was a big flag in front of the fire, and buried under that you had two horse's skulls to give it a nice drum effect for step dancing. Larry, when the humour took him, could knot the ankles in a horn-

75

pipe. Over the kitchen you had the loft, a recent renovation. There were no grants in those days and the money ran out, so there were only enough floor boards for what the bed stood on and about two feet of a runway in front of it. You had to watch the way you circumnavigated in and out of the bed or you might come down the near way to the kitchen.

Sitting below you would not be aware of the deficiency above for Larry's wife had opened out flour bags and tacked them up underneath the joists. It looked all right except that it was 'Bee Brand' flour they used to get, it was a bob or two less than 'Purity' or 'Prosperity', and if you remember there was a picture of a big bee walking up the side of the bag. When the bags were opened out, God Almighty! all the bees!

Now Larry's wife did her best to get the bees out of the bags. She boiled 'em in the pot, she danced on 'em in the river, but whatever indelible ink was in the print, she couldn't get the bees out of the bags. And I wouldn't mind but it was lovely cloth in those flour bags, gave great wear. Women used to make sheets out of it and little garments for themselves with 'Purity' in front and 'Prosperity' behind.

Larry's son that was sleeping above, and the same young Larry the devil or Doctor Reilly would not get him out of bed in the morning. The schoolmaster said he'd never be confirmed only that the catechism was at twelve o'clock in the day. If you saw him facing out for Mass on Sunday you'd turn home for you'd know you'd only have the soldier's part of it. Indeed people were saying would he be up in time for Mass in his own house?

Larry and his wife were up with the cock. They had to milk the cows, feed the calves and let out the horse. Then they called Lar. He'd be down in a minute! They put down a big *béiltigheach* of a fire in the kitchen and another in the grate in the room where the priest would have his breakfast. Then they called Lar. He'd be down in a minute. The bottle of whisky had to be put away where the priest wouldn't see it. Larry and the wife had to dress up to welcome the people, and indeed looking out the window they could see 'em making for the house so they called Lar.

Now one thing you'd want to be very careful of the morning of a station is wet paint. In the house where there is a smokey chimney, and Larry had one, paint don't dry. The dresser was varnished and the settle, even the chairs. That varnish was like birdlime and if, having sat on a chair, you got up out of it, you'd bring the chair all round the house with you.

The people sauntered in, and the two Cahilanes put their backs to the dresser, and stuck to it the same as you'd put a stamp on a letter. They were big quiet men that could remain motionless for a century. Now the parish priest that was there at the time was a trifle hasty, a little impatient and stern of demeanor, and signs by innocent people were peppering in dread of him. Although to go to the house you couldn't meet a nicer man. Jeremiah Horgan that was telling me, he was there for a letter of freedom, he was marrying some bird from an outside community. He got the letter — as things turned out he'd be better off if he didn't.

Big and all as Larry's kitchen was some of the neighbours waited in the yard. The morning turned out very dirty, but country people don't mind the rain — they say it never melted anyone. With that a son of Johnny Dan Thadhgeen's put his head around the corner of the cow house and said: 'He's coming!'

All the neighbours belted off into Larry's kitchen like lightning and left Larry there to welcome the parish priest. And Larry would rather any other job. He'd rather be draining the Dead Sea with a silver spoon for he was a very shy, distant sort of an individual.

In the kitchen when they heard the shout that the priest was coming the two Cahilanes went to go on their knees and brought the dresser down on top of 'em. There was an almighty crash of breaking delph which woke young Lar in the loft. He jumped out of bed and in his excitement overshot the runway. There was a tearing of flour bags and a scattering of bees and young Lar came sailing down between two rafters and sat on Hannah Maroya Casey's lap. . . a big red-faced woman getting her breath back after walking against the hill.

There he sat my *fostúach* of nineteen years of age with only a skimpy little shirt on him. The woman had to turn her face away. As she said to someone after, 'Indeed, I had something else on my mind, preparing myself for confession.'

By the time the dresser was put back on its feet and the sound side of the cups turned out, and young Lar had his clothes on, Father Mac came sailing into the yard holding over his head a black round roof on top of a walking cane.

78

This strange object left Larry speechless for that was the first umbrella that was seen in that quarter. Larry didn't say, 'Good morning' or 'Good day' or 'It was good of you to come', only took the horse and put him in the stable. Father Mac made off into the kitchen, and when those inside saw the doorway darkening all conversation faded like turning down the knob of the wireless, every man turned his back making himself small behind his neighbour in case any awkward question would be put to him.

When they turned around again, Father Mac had opened the umbrella at the bottom of the kitchen so as that the rain'd be running off it, and that it'd be nice and dry when he'd be going home by 'n' bye, that is when confessions'd be heard, Mass'd be said, breakfast'd be ate and dues'd be collected.

The morning wore on and all these things came to pass and the grace of God, glory be to Him, was in the house and Father Mac was in the room having his breakfast. The women were up and down to him, taking the legs off one another with excitement, and Larry's wife said and her face as red as a coal of fire, 'If you saw the look he gave me when he took the top off the egg!'

'Were they too done?' says Cáit.

'Bullets, girl! And I wouldn't mind, but I told that daughter of mine to watch 'em. But there you are the morning you'd want a thing to go right for you, that's the morning everything'd break the melt in you.'

The men were in the kitchen around the umbrella the same as if it was a German bomber. And they were saying that for such a simple thing, wasn't it a great wonder someone didn't think of it long 'go. And how handy it would be, they said, to prop it over the mouth of the barrel in the yard a wet day where you'd have a goose hatching. On the heel of that remark Father John came up from the room. They all backed toward the fire.

'Morning, men,' he said, 'what's the day doing?'

'Tis brightening, Father,' John Cronin said, a forward class of a man.

'I'll be going,' he said, 'there's many the thing I could be doing.'

'Good morning, Father,' they all said, and said it very loud and with great relief, for the bottle wouldn't be opened till he was gone.

Larry took the priest's horse from the stable and conveyed Father Mac down the passageway to the main road. They were nearly halfway down when Father Mac thought of his umbrella. 'Run up to the house,' he said to Larry, 'and bring me out my parasol.'

He didn't have to say this secondly. Larry ran up to the house and into the kitchen breathless. He took the umbrella by the leg, 'twas open, and brought it after him to the door, but it wouldn't go out. He came inside it and tried to shove it out before him, but the devil a out it'd go. He looked at those in the kitchen and they looked at him and they had pity on him. He took the door off the hinges — that'd give him an extra inch — but the umbrella wouldn't go out. Little beads of perspiration began to stand out on his forehead at the thought of Father Mac waiting in the passageway. He began muttering to himself, saying, 'If it came in, it must go out.'

Well, there was a small man there and, wanting to be of help, he said, 'I wonder would it be any value if we kicked out the two sides of the door frame?' The two sides of the frame were driven out in the yard, but the umbrella remained inside. 'Well,' says Larry, 'there's nothing for it now only knock down the wall.' A sledge hammer was procured and when Father Mac heard all the pounding, he doubled back to the house. And when he saw what was happening, 'twas as good as a tonic to him. He roared out laughing. 'What are you at?' says he. 'Well, do you know now, Father,' says Larry, 'I think myself that if I got the corner-stone there down, the mushroom'd sail out — no trouble.'

'Move into the kitchen from me,' says he. They did. Father Mac took the umbrella by the leg — 'twas open always — and brought it to the door in front of him. He was a fierce big man, God bless him, overcoat and all on a wet day, and they couldn't see what was happening. When he came to the door, like lightning he shut the umbrella and opened it again outside and walked out the yard holding it over his head, leaving them there spellbound.

When he was gone, Larry turned to his neighbours and said:

'Say what ye like, *they* have the power!'

CHAPTER FOURTEEN

CON AND BRIDGIE

There was this carpenter, and it would do your heart's good to see him working. Any sort of a fake-ah, no matter how complicated it was, if you could describe it to him he was able to make it, provided of course it was something in the building line. He couldn't make a clock or a mowing machine.

He was the first man around here to make a stand barrel churn. It was described to him by a man that saw one of 'em below in the county Limerick. And by all accounts he improved on the original, for he put a glass peephole in front of it so that you could see the entire operation going on inside.

He built a new house for Johnny Pa Pad. He built it around the old one, so that business could go on as usual. Johnny used to sell fishing tackle to the tourists and according to some of the lads the right man for it, a fly boy. He built the new house around the old one and when the new house was finished he threw the old one out the window.

The man was a marvel! And people were coming to him from all directions with every sort of a complicated contraption to have it copied or repaired. He told me himself, as a great secret, that the strangest request was from a woman, and I know if I tell it here it won't go any further.

She came one day to the workshop and looking around to see if the walls had ears she said to him:

'Could you make a division for a double bed?'

'And what form would it take?' says he.

'I don't know,' she said. 'Aren't you the carpenter. I suppose like a gate. Isn't that right, Con?' says she putting her head out around the corner of the door. 'A gate?'

'I don't know, Bridgie,' the husband was outside, 'you have me out of my mind yourself and that bed! Don't be dragging me into it!'

The carpenter thought then it might be an old fashioned camp bed they had. They were there when I was small, closed in on the three sides with a roof overhead. I don't know how people didn't smother inside in 'em. He thought maybe she wanted a gate to lock the children in. Children and all would be inside with the parents that time. If you looked down the room door you'd see all the little heads cocking out from under the quilt like chickens from under a hen's wing.

She said it was an ordinary wide double bed and she wanted a division in it. A gate.

'And where in the bed like!' he said. 'In the front?'

'No!' she said, 'in the middle.'

'Across?'

'No!' she said, 'up and down.' It would be very handy she explained to the carpenter if she could bring this thing into position before she'd go to sleep at night. But she wouldn't like it to be permanent. Could that be done?

He said it could, but that it would call for a lot of ingenuity!

She put her head around the corner of the door and said to her husband:

'It won't be permanent!'

The carpenter sat down, put on his thinking cap and began to draw lines on a piece of 11 in. x 1 in. deal board. He showed it to her saying:

'Maybe that'd do.'

She said it looked all right.

He made out a list of materials and told herself and the husband to go to Meagher's to get 'em and that he'd be over to the house Monday. Which he was.

He made a bench of the kitchen table and set to work. 3 in. x 1¼ in. scantlings he ordered. He thought they'd be strong enough, and he bridle-jointed the corners, 'twas the quickest, and in no time at all he had the gate made, 6 ft, 6 in. x 4 ft, 0 in. high with a diagonal stiffening piece. He came then, and if you saw the clever way he put two grooves, one at the top and one at the bottom of the bed, so that the division could slide up and down, for all the world like the sluice gate on a canal.

But that was not the beauty of it. He put two pulleys above in the rafters, and he ran a piece of sash cord from the top and bottom of the gate through the pulleys and on to two weights, and kept adding bits of lead to the weights until he achieved a perfect balance. There was one rope and Bridgie could pull the gate up with it, and then before she went to sleep at night there was another rope that she could take, and turning to Con she could say: 'Goodbye old faithful,' and pulling the rope bring the gate down between 'em.

He called the two of 'em down to see it working.

84

Bridgie was diverted, and Con could not get over the mechanics of it. Nothing would persuade him but that it was running on ballbearings, for all he had to do was put his finger under the gate and it would go up and down like a zip fastener.

The carpenter was well paid for his trouble and when he was going home Con conveyed him down a bit talking about this and that, and then he said:

'I suppose you are wondering why Bridgie wanted that fake-ah put in the bed?'

'I am a small bit curious,' says the carpenter.

'Well,' he said, 'it is this way and it is hard to believe it, but I was breaking in a young filly. I put the car on her; I was going to the Christmas Market with a butt of geese, a noisy cargo! Going up the road, whatever way it happened, a sheep to put his head around a gate pier, the horse bolted, went clean in over the ditch, and we fell ten feet into a field, myself and the geese and all. By the blessings of God we never capsised. The little mare did three rounds of the field, you'd swear it was Epsom and out the gap, but I got a great fright.

'When I came home that night I was telling the woman there. We went to bed anyway. . . Bridgie was between me and the wall. . . we were talking and then she fell asleep. I went to sleep too. What did I want awake for when there was no one to talk to? Out in the night I began to dream and this thing being in my mind about the fright I got that morning I dreamt that I was going with the young mare to bring a load of litter from the *muing*. Now, at the turn of the bridge there's a fierce declivity down into the *leaca* field. There were two dogs fighting and they rolled on to the road. The horse took fright and shot over the ditch and we fell down the declivity and were capsised. She was on the flat of her back, and you know she could kill herself kicking and she caught in the tackling. And the only thing to do in a case like that is to throw your whole weight down on her head.

'This I did and I caught her that way by the two ears. 'Wee, hoa, hack, stand up, aisy, aisy girl, stand up there!' With that I woke up. It was Bridgie's screeching woke me.

' "What are you at?" she said, "or will you take go of my ears. I'm smothered by you. I'll have to put a division in the bed if you don't give up your caffling!" And when it was the same thing the following night, Bridgie, as the man said, invoked the 1920 act and established partition.'

Not long after, Pádruig Ó Tuama of Coolea that was telling me, Con was capsised coming with a load of litter from the *muing*. He threw himself down of the horse's head until help came. They disentangled the mare from under the car. She was all right but Con wasn't. He gave his leg the hell of a bad twist, and Dr Carey said he blunted the nerve in the cup of the hip. He had no control over the movements of the leg. It made Dr Carey nervous to look at it and he said Con'd have to go up to the Mercy Hospital in Cork.

Con missed the train out of Loo Bridge station. He had to wait till the following day. Delays are dangerous then. Anyway he was kept above, and he hated the hospital, his first time away from Bridgie. No privacy there. People in and out, confined to bed when he needn't, food or nothing agreeing with him. 'Tis then, as he wrote in a long letter home to Bridgie, 'tis then you miss your own *bothán* where you can go where you like and do what you like and he wound up the letter with: 'I miss you, Bridgie, and I miss the brown bread and the pot under the bed!'

Bridgie wrote back to him. 'You won't miss me long more for I'm going up to see you Friday and you won't miss the brown bread for I'm bringing two cakes of it with me, and as for the pot under the bed, well, Con, you always missed that.'

When Con was discharged from the hospital he missed the train home. He was in a pub late that night and the place was raided. They all cleared out the back way and into a graveyard, where Con fell into an open grave. He was wedged at the bottom, I suppose he had too much drink in to get up. It was the coldest night that ever came and it wasn't long until he began calling:

'Help, help! Lift me up, I'm perished. I'm dying with the cold!'

A drunk crept to the edge of the grave. The moon was shining and when he saw Con on the flat of his back he said:

'No bloody wonder you'd be cold and you having all the clay kicked off yourself!'

The seagulls screaming in the morning woke Con. He stood up in the grave and people say that it was his first time ever seeing the dawn. The slanting sun shining through the headstones was a strange sight. When his eyes became accustomed to the light he saw many more open graves around him and lifting his eyes to heaven he said:

'Oh Lord, don't tell me it is the resurrection and I've missed that too.'

They went the lower road I came the high road, they crossed by the stepping stones I came over the bridge, they were drowned and I was saved, but all I ever got out of my storytelling was shoes of brown paper and stockings of thick milk, I only know what I heard, I only heard what was said and a lot of what was said was gospel!

GLOSSARY

For the benefit of the readers unfamiliar with the Irish language this list of Irish words (or words derived from Irish) is appended. In translating we have endeavoured not only to give verbal equivalences but also to convey something of the flavour of the meaning of the original Irish.

A mhic ó — sonny

Bothán — little hut
Ball Seirce — a love or beauty spot
Béiltigheach — a great fire

Cábúis — nook
Cábúisín — little nook
Craínín — scythe sharpener
Caoining — lamenting
Ciseán — basket
Croí an diail (diabhail) — by the devil's heart
Caipín — cap
Ceithearnach — local tyrant, or one who aped the English

Fostúach — hireling/grown lad (derogatory, a lump of a boy)

Gabhál — held in the arms
Grafán — a grubber

Is tuísce deoch ná sceál — a drink first and then a story

Joeyman — fairy

Leaca — field at base of hillside

Muing — grassy swamp

Ní nach ionadh — no wonder

Poitín — poteen

Peidhleachán — butterfly

Smathán — a small quantity
Stór — love (term of endearment)
Seadh — yes
Spailpín — a migratory farm labourer
Slán mar a n-ínnstear é — God bless the hearers
Seanchaí — storyteller
Seanchaithe — storytellers
Swee gee — a turn, twist

Teasbach — energy
Tulc — spasm, fit of laughter.